WHERE DID ALL THE RHINOS GO?

WRITTEN BY LARA JACKSON

ILLUSTRATED BY KELLY ULRICH

INSPIREBYTES OMNI MEDIA

Where Did All The Rhinos Go?

Distributed globally with Expanded Distribution by KDP.

ISBN Paperback: 978-1-953445-14-8
ISBN ebook: 978-1-953445-15-5
LCCN: 2021944434

⧮ INSPIREBYTES OMNI MEDIA

Inspirebytes Omni Media LLC
PO Box 988
Wilmette, IL 60091

For more information, please visit www.inspirebytes.com.

FOR IAN.

You protected the rhinos and patrolled the skies.
You were a ray of sunshine in the world of conservation,
and the light of your legacy will shine on.

In the land of Africa, that's not so far away,
Animals lived in balance, predators among prey.

1

Antelopes and zebras dotted the plains,
Giraffes tall as trees and lions with big manes.
Spotted cats ran faster than any breeze,
And large, slithering snakes rustled through leaves.

2

They roamed the savannahs, eating along the way,
Searching for cool waters to drink and to play.
Where hippos would wallow in pools of brown mud,
And buffalos collided with a mighty THUD!

3

But since those times, a lot has changed,
The plains are mostly empty, and the silence feels strange.

More and more humans are living on the land,
Their towns, roads, and cities continue to expand.
The wildlife is disappearing as there's no longer room,
For all the animals to live and the flowers to bloom.

So now, there is *one* thing that I really wish to know,
An answer to the question: where did all the rhinos go?

The little black rhino sat all alone,
He let out a whimper, followed by a groan.
The poachers had come late in the night,
They'd taken his mama, though she'd put up a fight.

Why they took her,
he wasn't quite sure,
Was it something to do with
the horn that she wore?

Although he felt sad,
he knew what to do,
He must find the others,
even though there were few.

7

For days and days, he marched in the sun,
But he didn't see a rhino, not even one.
Once he saw monkeys munching on fruit,
But no other animals walked the same route.

8

Suddenly a bird flew down from above,
Dark brown in colour with a beak red as blood.

"Hello little rhino, may I perch on your back?
It's okay! Don't be scared, all I want is a snack!
I'll eat all the insects and ticks from your skin,
I promise it won't hurt; can I begin?"

"Mr. Oxpecker, you seem very smart,
Can I ask a question before you start?
I must find the others, so I need to know,
Where did all the rhinos go?"

10

"Oh child, I'm sorry, I know you're alone,
It's a mystery to me that remains unknown.
We've noticed there are fewer rhinos around,
I perched on many friends who can no longer be found."

"I know of an elephant who lives in the west,
I'm sure she'll be able to help with your quest.
For they are the wisest animals by far,
And their memories last as long as the stars."

"She's not far away, at most two days,
But now little one, we must part ways."

The little rhino wandered, alone once again,
Until he walked past a hyena den.

Two of them emerged
with a gleeful snicker,
And although he ran, they
were so much quicker!

13

They circled around him, drool dripping from their chins,
But then they revealed their huge toothy grins.

"Don't worry little rhino, we don't eat your kind,
You're far from home, what are you trying to find?"

"My Mama* was taken,
so I need to know,
Where did all the rhinos go?"

The hyenas looked stunned as they licked their muzzles,

"Just give us a moment to think on this puzzle.
We haven't seen a rhino for months... or years!
But why on earth would they just disappear?"

15

"We don't really know where the rhinos are,
Though we're sure you won't need to journey too far.
Now little one, you should go on your way,
We'll always be here if you return some day."

Through the open savannahs dotted with trees,
He thought about where the elephants could be.
He passed zebra herds with frolicking foals,
And saw animals drinking from blue waterholes.

17

Then, one day as he crested a hill,
His heart leapt inside him; he couldn't keep still!
There were large grey animals resting in the grass,
The little rhino had found the elephants at last!

18

Weaving through legs as thick as trees,
Amongst the herd, he yelled,

"Excuse me, please!"

"I must find the others, so I need to know,
Where did all the rhinos go?"

19

"For the rhinos have disappeared year upon year,
As they hide in the bush and cower in fear.
A terrible storm has covered the land,
And today rhinos are dying by human hands."

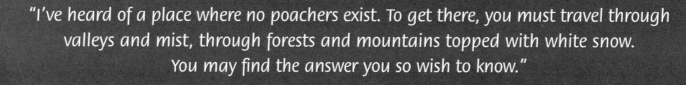

"I've heard of a place where no poachers exist. To get there, you must travel through valleys and mist, through forests and mountains topped with white snow. You may find the answer you so wish to know."

"Now young one, you should go on your way, But we'll be your family if you want to stay."

Finally some hope to carry him at last,
He was so close to the answer, he had to be fast.

Sneaking past a leopard
dozing in a tree,
The little rhino ran as
fast as the breeze.

Suddenly there was a crack
from behind a spiky bush,
A human girl emerged, and
she told him to *shuuuush*.

"My name is Kesi. I won't hurt you, don't worry,
But the poachers aren't far, we really must hurry."

Deep in the shadows, they travelled through the night,
They didn't dare relax until the dawn of first light.

As the world around them was warmed by the sun,
They took a deep breath; a new day had begun.

"My Baba* was a bush pilot before he died,
He protected the rhinos and patrolled the skies.
He told me to care for nature's beauty,
And saving the rhinos is now my duty."

With that, the little rhino felt so sad and so small,
As he hung his head and let the tears fall.

*Baba = father in Swahili

"You shouldn't feel sad,
for it's not just you,
We humans are doing it
to other animals too."

And as they travelled through lands unknown,
She told him of the havoc that people had sown.

"My Baba has told me of the great orangutan,
Large and orange like a giant hairy man.
We're destroying their home, the trees in which they swing,
Once the pride of the rainforest, they're no longer the king."

28

"At the top of the world lies the land of the cold,
Where huge, white bears wander, wild and bold.
But humans have caused the earth to warm,
So, the ice the bears live on no longer forms."

"And deep in the sea, large animals used to swim,
But the waters are full of waste, rope tangling their limbs."

"Sea turtles are eating plastic instead of jellyfish,
Oh, I would clean up the oceans, if I had one wish."

"In the open meadows where wildflowers thrive,
The bees are always busy, collecting pollen for their hives.
But humans use bad chemicals to help their crops grow,
And it's hurting the bees, now their numbers are low."

"So, you see little rhino, it isn't just you,
We're watching other animals disappear, too.
I know it doesn't help that your problem is shared,
But have hope, there are so many good people who care."

So lost in his thoughts, he didn't even see,
The changes in the land and the thinning of the trees.
Suddenly they stumbled into a large open space,
After days of travelling, they'd found the safe place!

They stared in disbelief at what they could see,
There were hundreds of animals, all wandering free.
But one in particular caught their eye,
With horns so large, they nearly reached the sky.

Together they sprinted across the plains,
Their joy and excitement couldn't be contained.

Weaving their way through the rhinos in the crowd,
They found the lead female, majestic, and proud.

35

She bowed before them, lowering her horns,
To another orphan whose mother she would mourn.

"Excuse me Bibi*, I've journeyed far to find you.
Why was Mama taken, can you give me a clue?"

*Bibi = grandmother in Swahili

"Oh, my poor dear, there's something you must hear.
  Come closer and listen, I'll whisper in your ear."

"Our horns became wanted long, long ago,
  Taken to faraway lands on ships to-and-fro.
  To where people believed our horns held magical powers,
  And they wanted to take them even though they were ours."

"Now even today, though science has shown,
That they are not magic—as we've always known—
We are still hunted until we are few,
If only we could tell them, if only they knew."

38

"That our horns are the same as the nail on their toe,
Science can prove it; it's always been so.
Unless they can learn and stop their ways,
There will be no more rhinos at the end of their days."

"But now you are safe, so
come rest in the shade,
And never let the memory
of your Mama fade.
For here we can be together
and live happily,
From now on, little rhino,
we are your family."

40

Today, the last rhinos are protected by wonderful rangers,
Who work hard to keep them safe from all of the dangers.
But we really need your help to keep spreading the word;
Will you stand up for rhinos? Let your voices be heard?

Or do you know of other animals that
need your help, too?
If so, have a think, what else can you do?

Could you talk to your family, or even your friends,
To share all these stories, and change how they end?

If we use our voice for those who can't speak,
Then the future of our planet won't be so bleak.
For if we create more wild spaces and make more room,
Then the wildlife can live, and the flowers can bloom.

43

ABOUT THE AUTHOR
LARA JACKSON

Lara is a conservation biologist and wildlife photographer whose research has taken her all around the world!

She believes that raising awareness and increasing engagement is the key to successful conservation efforts. Lara is determined to use her camera as a voice for the voiceless and continue telling the stories of those who work tirelessly to conserve some of the most endangered species on the planet.

You can find Lara on instagram at: @lara_wildlife

ABOUT THE ILLUSTRATOR
KELLY ULRICH

Kelly is an artist from the west coast of British Columbia, Canada. She is a lover of nature and paints pictures of the deep, green ocean and misty forests she lives near.

Currently, there is a family of Steller's Jays that visit Kelly in her art studio looking for peanuts, and every morning she feeds the two fish that live in a rain barrel. When not watching the squirrels, raccoons, one rat, and the hummingbirds from her balcony, she is working on her cartoon series, Dean & Nala + Vinny, on Instagram.

You can find Kelly on Instagram at: @kellyulrichartist

A NOTE FROM LARA AND KELLY
Supporting Rhino Conservation

There are five rhino species in the world and all of them are in trouble. I (Lara) feel very privileged to have worked closely with black rhinos in Kenya, alongside some of the most determined, passionate, and amazing conservationists and rangers. I can honestly say that there are so many people out there who care, working incredibly hard to conserve this magnificent animal.

By purchasing this book, you'll be helping rhino conservation efforts around the globe, as 10% of profits from each sale will be donated to Save The Rhino and/or other charities working tirelessly to raise awareness for this amazing species. Together we can make a difference, together we can reverse the tide, and together, we can save the rhino.

Lara and Kelly

The amazing rangers of Lewa Wildlife Conservancy & Borana Conservancy helping Lara with her rhino research in Kenya.

Ian with Kitui, an orphaned black rhino calf at Lewa Wildlife Conservancy, Kenya. Here, Ian was being an oxpecker and was removing any ticks and insects from Kitui's skin!

QUESTIONS TO HELP START A CONVERSATION

1. Do you know what poaching is?

2. Can you think of any other animals that might be affected by poaching?

3. In the book we learned that humans are also cutting down the trees where orangutans live and using chemicals for their crops that hurt the bees. Can you think of other ways that humans are negatively affecting wildlife?

4. Change can begin at home. What can you do to help the wildlife in your garden survive?

5. How do you think we can help the rhino and other animals that live far away from us?

When searching for black rhinos, you often find the wrong species! Here is Lara's research partner Dickson Mure in front of three white rhinos that they spotted during their research! The white rhinos are much further away than they look!

Lara & her research partner David Mbusia collecting data in Lewa Wildlife Conservancy, Kenya.

RESOURCES TO LEARN MORE

If you'd like to learn more about how you can help the rhinos, here are some of Lara's favorite resources:

• www.savetherhino.org/rhino-info/rhino-kids/

• www.actionforrhinos.com/education.html

• www.helpingrhinos.org/rhinocation/

• www.rhinoresourcecenter.com

Where Did All The Rhinos Go? is part of an ongoing series of children's books on conservation. To learn more about different work going on around the world to help our animal friends and our planet, visit www.conservation4kids.com.

Lara with Kitui, an orphaned black rhino calf at Lewa Wildlife Conservancy in Kenya. Kitui was taken into care at just a few weeks of age and was hand-raised by an incredible team of rangers.

A truly magical encounter with three white rhinos and one of Lara's favourite memories with these gentle giants. Lara was taking photos of the rhinos grazing and before she knew it, all three had wandered over and were eating a mere ten metres from her!

Made in the USA
Las Vegas, NV
03 October 2021